Little Elfie One

By **Pamela Jane**   Illustrated by **Jane Manning**

BALZER + BRAY

An Imprint of HarperCollinsPublishers

Balzer + Bray is an imprint of HarperCollins Publishers.

Little Elfie One

Text copyright © 2015 by Pamela Jane

Illustrations copyright © 2015 by Jane Manning

All rights reserved. Manufactured in China.

ISBN 978-0-06-220673-2

This artist used Winsor & Newton watercolors on Lanaquarelle
140 cold-press paper to create the illustrations for this book.
Typography by Rachel Zegar
15 16 17 18 19   SCP   10 9 8 7 6 5 4 3 2 1
❖
First Edition

To Nancy Gump, my creative writing buddy,
and George Arrick, our incomparable teacher and friend

—P.J.

For Tatiana with love

—J.M.

Way up in the North
        Where the reindeer run
A big mommy elf
        Called her little elfie one.

"Santa comes tomorrow!"
"Hooray!" cried the one.
And he leaped and he laughed
Where the reindeer run.

Way up in the North

Where the ice shines blue

Lived a furry father mouse

And his little mousies two.

"Nibble!" said the father;

"We nibble," said the two.

And they gnawed and they nibbled

Where the ice shines blue.

Way up in the North
On a festive fir tree
Hung a gingerbread daddy
And his little gingies three.

"Run!" cried the daddy;

"We run," cried the three.

And they hopped down and ran

From the festive fir tree.

Way up in the North
　　Came a knock upon the door.
Surprise! A mother caroler
　　And her little carolers four!

"Sing!" cried the mother;
　　"We sing," said the four.
So they sang songs of joy
　　By the little elfie's door.

Way up in the North
    Where the polar bears dive
Lived an old mommy polar
    And her little polies five.

"Swim!" cried the mommy;
    "We swim," cried the five.
And they swam and they splashed
    Where the polar bears dive.

Way up in the North
     Near a barn built of sticks
Lived a big daddy snowman
     And his little snowies six.

"Shiver!" said the daddy;
     "We shiver," said the six.
So they shivered and they shook
     Near the barn built of sticks.

Way up in the North
In the dark starry heaven
Lived a bright mother star
And her little starries seven.

"Wink!" said the mother;
"We wink," said the seven.
So they winked and they blinked
In the dark starry heaven.

Way up in the North
    It was growing very late!
So old Father Santa
    Called his little helpers eight.

"Hurry!" said Santa;
    "We hurry," said the eight.
And they hurried and they scurried
    So they would not be late!

Way up in the North
　　　Near a tall snowy pine
Old Father Santa called
　　　His little reindeer nine.

"Fly!" cried Santa;
　　　"We fly," cried the nine.
And they sailed and they soared
　　　O'er the tall snowy pine.

Way up in the North
 In a warm cozy den
Lived a gray mommy cat
 And her little kittens ten.

"Frolic!" said the mother;
 "We frolic," said the ten.
So they frisked and they frolicked
 In the warm cozy den.

Way up in the North
    Where the reindeer run
The big mommy elf
    Called her little elfie one.

"There he goes!" cried the mommy;
"Merry Christmas!" called the one.

Santa winked. "I'll be back

For some Merry Christmas fun!"